The Case of
The Long-Lost Twin

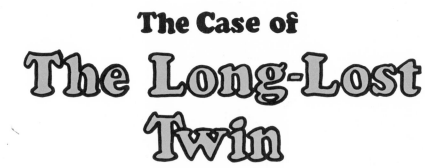

by **Dan Cohen** ✦ *Pictures by* **George Overlie**

CAROLRHODA BOOKS
MINNEAPOLIS, MINNESOTA U S A

1 2 3 4 5 6 7 8 9 10 85 84 83 82 81 80 79

"Poor Wilma," said Officer Grover Greenwood. "If it isn't one thing, it's another. She must be awfully upset."

"What do you mean, Officer Greenwood?" asked Ruthann. Ruthann and her little sister, Polly, were Officer Greenwood's special friends. They had helped him solve several of his most difficult cases. He always stopped to chat with them when they ran into each other. They often met at the Spring Grove Ice Cream Shop. Officer Greenwood liked ice cream almost as much as Ruthann and Polly did. But this time he didn't order his favorite treat, a banana split.

"Aren't you having anything?" Polly asked him. Officer Greenwood could see a little bit of chocolate ice cream on one side of Polly's mouth. There was a little bit of whipped cream on the other. Having an ice cream mess on her face didn't seem to bother Polly at all.

"No," said Officer Greenwood, groaning. "The Chief said I've got to lose thirty pounds in the next three months or he'll take me off the force. Besides, I'm too worried about my friend Wilma to think about ice cream." He tried not to watch Polly as she stuffed a giant spoonful of banana split into her mouth.

"What's it all about?" asked Ruthann.

"Well, you remember that Wilma worked for many years as a housekeeper to Miss Tromly. It was a real blow to her when Miss Tromly died last month. Wilma thought she'd have no job and no place to go. She was getting on in years, too. Life can be very hard for a person in that situation," said Officer Greenwood.

"But I thought everything had turned out all right," said Ruthann. "Mom and Dad told me that Miss Tromly had left a letter for Wilma. The letter said that Wilma would receive some money and very valuable things in return for all her kindness and years of work."

"That's what we all thought," said Officer Greenwood, "but it turns out that might not be so. You see, I guess Miss Tromly had a twin sister. She hadn't been heard from for years, until now. I hear she's got a will of Miss Tromly's, leaving everything to her. Now poor Wilma will get nothing."

After Officer Greenwood left, Ruthann and Polly decided to go over and visit Wilma. Maybe they could cheer her up. She was living in a rooming house that wasn't nearly as nice as the house she had lived in when Miss Tromly was alive. Even though she seemed happy to see her two friends, Ruthann could tell she had been crying.

A few minutes after the girls arrived, there was a knock on the door. Wilma opened it to find a very large grey-haired woman.

"May I help you?" asked Wilma.

"Yes, you certainly may," said the woman. "My, what a . . . er . . . interesting little place you have here. My name is Fran Tromly Hoople. I'm Fan Tromly's twin sister. Now, dear, I hear you have been making trouble for me. This simply has got to stop. I don't want to hurt you. But if you don't start to behave yourself, well, I may have to get a teeny weeny bit unpleasant."

"What do you mean?" asked Wilma.

"Oh, I think you know. You are trying to get my sister's money. But it's rightfully mine." She waved an official-looking paper in front of Wilma. "Here's a will that poor Fan sent to

me just before she died, leaving all her money
to me. Fan and I may not have been very close
over the years, but after all, we *were* sisters.
In fact, here's a picture of the two of us to-
gether as children."

The woman pulled out a faded yellow newspaper clipping. It showed two smiling children. They didn't look very much alike. But both had short, curly dark hair, and both were dressed in plaid summer shirts and shorts. They were holding hands. Under the picture it said, "The Tromly twins, Fan and Fran, both won their races at the Fourth of July picnic yesterday."

Ruthann studied the picture closely. There was something a little strange about it. But she couldn't quite figure out what it was. She memorized the date, just in case, and handed the picture back to the woman.

"I knew Fan Tromly had a twin named Fran, but she never talked about it. I always thought her twin was dead," said Wilma.

The Tromly twins, Fan and Fran, both won their races on the Fourth of July picnic yesterday.

"You see how little you really know about my family, dear? I'm afraid that just shows you are not entitled to any money. But I'm not a mean person. I want to help you, you poor dear thing. I'll give you a thousand dollars. All you have to do is just sign this paper."

"What does it say?" asked Wilma.

"It says that you will give up your claim to the money and turn over any rights you have to me."

"I'm not sure I should sign this."

"If you don't sign it, you'll get nothing. In fact, less than nothing. Because I'll get my lawyer after you. We'll sue you and take away everything you've got left, just for being such a bother," said the woman.

"Oh, girls, what am I to do?" cried Wilma.

"You have until tomorrow to decide," said the visitor, heading for the door. "I'll be back at noon. And your answer had better be yes!" The door slammed.

Wilma began to cry.

"Gee, Wilma, that lady sure was mean," said Polly. "Even Ruthann has never been that mean to me."

"I have an idea, Wilma," said Ruthann. "As long as we have until tomorrow, maybe there is something we can do. Cm'on, Polly."

Ruthann and Polly left. They promised to return in time for the meeting the next day. But instead of going straight home, Ruthann made Polly stop at the library with her.

"Where can we find old newspapers on file?" Ruthann asked the librarian. When she found out, she went right to the file that held the newspaper for the date of the clipping that the large woman had shown her. It took only a minute to find out what she wanted to know.

"Cm'on, Polly," said Ruthann. "We're going to find Officer Greenwood."

The next day, Ruthann and Polly went to
Wilma's apartment a little before noon. At
exactly 12 o'clock, there was a knock on the
door. It was the "long-lost twin."

"Well, Wilma," she said. "Don't look so nervous. It isn't every day that someone offers you a thousand dollars to sign your name." She seemed very pleased with herself. She handed Wilma the paper to sign. Just then Officer Greenwood stepped out of the little kitchen where he had been waiting.

"I don't think anybody will be doing any signing today," said Officer Greenwood. "Or any other day, for that matter."

"Who are you? What are you talking about?" asked the visitor.

"I'm Officer Grover Greenwood. But *you're* certainly not Fan Tromly's twin!"

"How do you know?" the "twin" asked. Her face was getting very red.

"Because Fran Tromly was a man, not a woman," said Officer Greenwood.

j39951

"Something about that picture you showed us wasn't right," said Ruthann. "Of course, I could see right away that the two weren't identical twins. They were fraternal twins. That means that one could be a boy and one a girl. Then I noticed that their shirts looked different. One buttoned from the right, and the other buttoned from the left. Then, I remembered that boys and girls button their shirts from different sides!"

"When Ruthann went to the library, she found out where you got that picture. You said you'd been carrying it around for years," said Officer Greenwood. "But you really cut it out of the library's newspaper file. The librarian said someone had been looking in that file only last week. Someone who looked just like you."

The "twin" swallowed hard. "I thought I had it all figured out. I had the same first name as Fan Tromly's brother. Of course, I spelled mine Frances, and his was Francis. When Fan died, I thought how easy it would be to pretend I was her twin. I knew that the real twin could never claim Fan's money."

"I'm way ahead of you," said Officer Green-wood. "Our police files show that the real Fran Tromly died in prison twenty years ago. He and your husband were cellmates. That's why Fan never talked about her twin brother." The woman sank into a chair and wiped her forehead.

"Impersonating someone is a serious matter," said Officer Greenwood. "And I'm sure that when we do some checking, we'll find out that the 'will' you have is a fake. I think you'd better come with me to police headquarters."

When Wilma realized what had happened, she was overjoyed. She was so grateful to Officer Greenwood and the two girls that she invited them to a little party in her apartment. After Officer Greenwood had taken the woman to police headquarters, he came back and joined in. Wilma brought out chocolate ice cream and cookies. She made some coffee for Officer Greenwood.

As the girls ate their ice cream, they talked about the case they had just solved.

"You know, that woman wasn't a very good criminal," said Ruthann. "She even left another clue."

"What was that?" asked Polly. She already had chocolate dripping down her chin.

"She forgot to cut out the story in the paper that went along with the picture," said Ruthann. "It told how Fan Tromly won the *girls'* 100-yard dash, and Fran Tromly won the *boys'* half-mile race!"

"You mean boys used to be afraid to run against girls in the olden days?" asked Polly.

"Something like that," said Officer Greenwood. He looked at Polly and wondered if maybe just *one* little scoop of ice cream wouldn't be all right.